Dalmatian Press, 2007. All rights reserved. Printed in the U.S.A. 1-866-418-2572
The DALMATIAN PRESS name, logo, and Tear and Share are trademarks of Dalmatian Publishing Group, LLC, Franklin, Tennessee 37067.
No part of this book may be reproduced or copied in any form without written permission from the copyright owner.

09 10 B&M 34955 12 11 10
16290 Power Rangers 8x8 - Operation Overdrive: Operation Teamwork

Throughout the history of Mankind, good has battled evil. Now dark forces once again have arisen to overpower the world. Two brothers, Flurious and Moltor, each seek the five lost jewels of the Corona Aurora—jewels that will bestow ultimate power to the wearer! Yet two things stand in their way: their own hatred for each other...

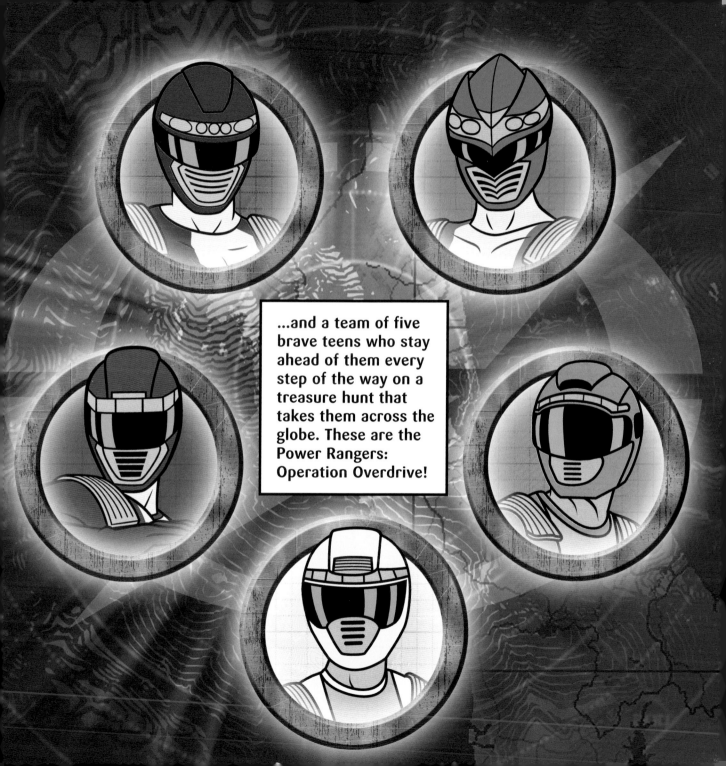

...and a team of five brave teens who stay ahead of them every step of the way on a treasure hunt that takes them across the globe. These are the Power Rangers: Operation Overdrive!

Mack, the Red Ranger, is the gung-ho leader of the group. As a Ranger, he has incredible super strength. His billionaire dad, Andrew Hartford, directs the team on their missions.

Dax, the Blue Ranger, is an international stuntman. His Ranger skill is super leaping and bounce-back ability. Nothing keeps him down!

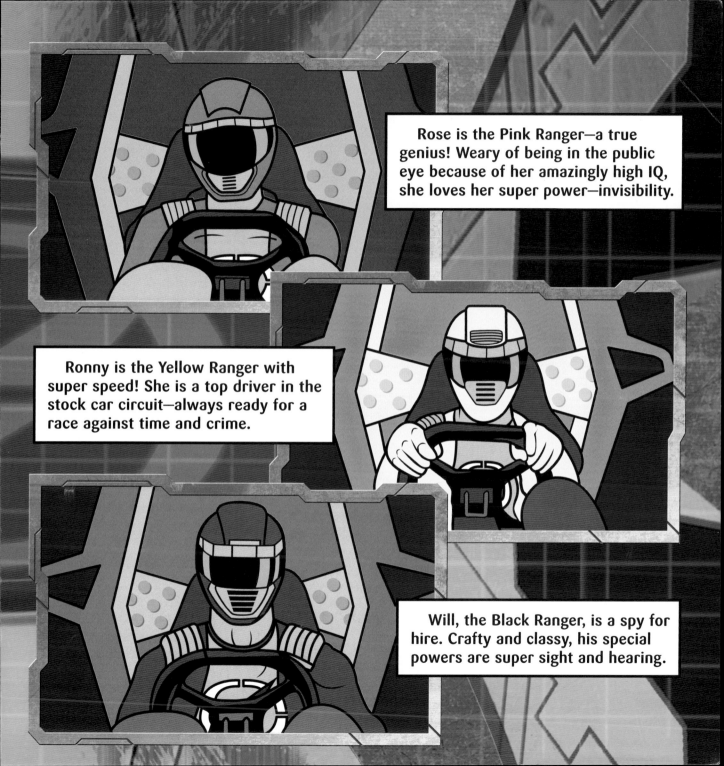

Deep in his Ice Den, Flurious was furious with his assistant, Norg.

"I sent you out to look for the Corona Aurora jewels, and yet you return with nothing! Find my jewels before the Rangers..."

Just then a sonic boom rattled the Ice Den. It was the Power Rangers' Shark vehicle—right above them!

Moltor appeared on Flurious's screen. "Flurious!" he demanded. "Any sign of the Rangers?"

"Why, no, brother," responded Flurious with a sly grin. "Nothing at all. But I'll be sure to call you..."

Flurious raised his staff and sent a blizzard swirling around the Shark. But this was not going to stop the Rangers! They had been sent on a special mission to retrieve one of the jewels from the ancient city of Atlantis, deep under the sea. The blizzard rocked the Shark, but they landed safely on shore.

Will, the Black Ranger, sent a message through his Tracker back to home base: "Send the Zords!"

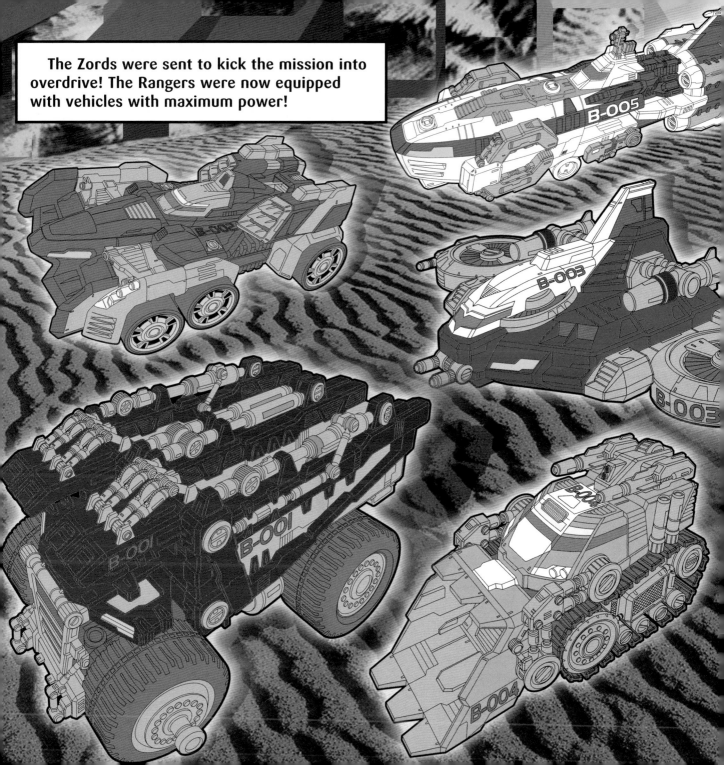

The Zords were sent to kick the mission into overdrive! The Rangers were now equipped with vehicles with maximum power!

Piloted by the Pink Ranger, the Aqua Drive Zord raced toward their destination, with Will and Ronny manning the co-pilot stations.

Up ahead loomed the ruins of Atlantis!
Mack, the Red Ranger, came up on the viewing screen. "Be careful, guys. Those ruins are 10,000 years old. You're looking for the great temple. The jewel should be inside."

Will and Ronny headed toward the ruins using their hand-held propellers. They emerged from the water, deep inside the ruins—and stumbled onto a secret chamber.

"Looks like we found the temple," said Will.

Behind a hidden door they found an illuminated cocoon with a high Tracker reading.

Just then, Mack and Dax arrived on the scene.

"Mack!" cried Will. "I have this under control. I'll take the cocoon. I like to work alone."

"Will!" called Mack. "You're not the only person on this team!"

"Maybe I should be!" Will called back, running farther into the cave—with Mack on his heels.

But as Will struggled, trying to open the cocoon, it slipped from his hands and rolled to the edge of a cliff. Will dove after it. As he grabbed the cocoon, he fell over the side, holding onto the edge with only one hand.

"Will! Give me the cocoon!" said Mack. "I'll pull you up!"

"No... I can... do it..." gasped Will.

"Will! Let me help you," said Mack.
"We're a team."

Will stared up at Mack. He knew Mack
was right. He handed the cocoon to Mack,
and Mack grabbed his free hand, pulling
him to safety. It was a close call.

As Mack and Will emerged from the cave, they encountered their team battling Flurious and his foot soldiers—Chillers!

"Drive Defender!" called Mack.

The Rangers drew their weapons, which transformed into lasers and swords.

"Give me the jewel!" roared Flurious. He raised his staff—and suddenly the entire temple came to life! "Rise and defeat the Power Rangers!"

The Rangers fell to the ground as the earth shook. The Temple of Atlantis stood like a huge machine—filled with Flurious's fury!

"Any ideas?" asked Dax.

"Yeah," answered Mack, pulling out his Tracker. "It's Zord time!"

The Zords, commanded by the Rangers, moved in to blast the monster Temple.

"Rev 'em up! Fire!" they called together.

"You guys take the lead," cried Will.

"It's gotta be a team effort, Will," said Ronny.

"All for one, and one for all!" cheered Dax. "Dig this!"

The Zords fired rockets and blasted the huge Temple, yet it did not fall.

"Let's combine!" called Mack. "Drivemax Megazord!"
The Rangers engaged their morphers and the Zords
transformed into the mighty Megazord.
"Operation Overdrive!"

The Megazord slammed a pickaxe into the ground, blasting the Temple Monster.

"That got him!" cried Will.

But just then, the Monster stepped forward and grabbed the Overdrive Megazord!

"What now?" called Rose.

"Aim for his power core!" said Mack.

"Right!" answered Rose. "Activating Drivemax Saber Combination!"

The Megazord transformed the pickaxe and the shovel into the Power Sword. The Monster tried to grab the sword, but with one powerful sweep, the sword felled the evil giant—sending it crashing to the ground and exploding into a million pieces.

Defeated and deflated, Flurious retreated back to his icy lair—to plot and plan his next villainous move....

Back at headquarters, the Rangers gathered around the cocoon.
   "Let's open this up and see which lost jewel of the Corona Aurora we've found," said Mack.
   "One powerful jewel coming up!" said Rose.
   But the cocoon opened to reveal an ancient bamboo scroll.
   "What do you think is inside the scroll?" asked Dax.
   "Only one way to find out," said Ronny. "Pop that puppy open."

The scroll opened to reveal the next piece of the puzzle....

"Cool!" said Rose. "It's the Sword of Neptune. Time for research and..."

"Our next mission!" said Max. "Ready, team?" He looked at Will.

"Ready!" said Will, smiling. "All for one, and one for all!"